Steve Warrior

Table of Contents

D1411074

Mundane Monday

It has been a few years since I started living on my own. The only thing I brought with me when I moved here was this book and quill. After settling in and getting to know the place I finally decided to start writing in here. So, my book and quill, my name is Steve. I hope we will experience many great adventures together. Today is just a normal every day Monday. Not much to write about so how about I start with introducing my village.

I live in a small developing village in the savanna. We are right on the edge of the ocean and have a great source of fish. We also have a mountain nearby that provides us with minerals. Our farms are mostly filled with potatoes as it is our village's favorite food. I can make a great baked potato! We also have some carrots and wheat growing as well. We used to have some beetroot growing but some kids that hated it decided to go and jump on them.

There is a church that I sometimes go to. The priest likes to teach everyone how to be good citizens. Although most of the time, I doze off during those lectures. Sometimes he will also teach us fun things like how to use a bow or how to bake yummy bread. I am bad at hitting the target but I love eating bread.

We have a library filled with great books to read and a friendly librarian that acts as the teacher of the village. He teaches all the kids' stuff like how to read and speak. He also teaches the history of the world. Back in the day everyone used to just make sounds to communicate.

There is also a blacksmith that helps provide the villagers with weapons and armor to fight against any invasions that might happen. Since being here, I have only seen a couple of zombies roam close by. The

village seems to have been placed in a fairly safe area. The blacksmith gave me a wooden sword as a moving in present and helped me in crafting a shield. He taught me how to fight with the sword and shield so that I can become a warrior to protect this village.

Now let me end my village tour with my favorite place in the entire village, my house! It is a little plain still but I got all the necessities: a bed, chests to put my stuff into,

4

a furnace to cook my baked potatoes, and a bookshelf for my books. I also went swimming for some clay and made my very own flowerpot. After picking a flower I placed it inside but it died rather quick. I still never got around to replacing it. My window gives a great view of the water. An even better view is the one from my roof. I built a ladder on the side of my house so I can go up there from time to time. Sometimes I just like to sit up there and watch the stars. I am actually writing in here while sitting up here now. It is another beautiful morning for fishing so I will write again tonight about what I caught.

Back from another normal day in the village. I caught a couple of raw salmon so I am cooking those up now. It is good to have a variety of food instead of the usual baked potato. I also fished up some rotten flesh that I quickly fed to the squids. One of those zombies must have died down there, how disturbing. At least the squids seemed to enjoy it. The priest told me not to feed them or they are going to keep hanging around for more, like those wolves bagging for bones. Sometimes they can get in the way of fishing. I, personally, do not mind their company. I hope I fish out a bone sometime too so I can feed the wolves as well.

After fishing, I went on a walk around the village. A lot of the villagers like asking me to help them with variety of things. The first villager asked me to help plow the land that the kids have ruined. The second villager asked me to cut down a tree that was in the way. I got to keep the wood so I could fuel my furnace or craft stuff with it. The third villager asked me to shovel some dirt that blocked the door to his house. How did the dirt get there in the first place? Then the blacksmith asked me to help him smelt some iron ore into iron bars. He made me an iron sword with some iron, to replace my worn out wooden sword that he gave me when I moved in. It was a sword practice graduation gift he told me. I thanked him and continued on my walk around the village.

It was getting dark now and the priest was telling everyone to go inside. I went and climbed the church to take a look around. I really wanted to test out my new sword. That was when I heard a loud boom. Was it someone playing around with TNT or was this the work of a creeper? I saw the hole that the explosion made just outside the village. Luckily nobody was hurt. Then I saw a creeper coming out of that hole. If that hole came from a creeper, why did it suddenly explode? He was going towards one of the villager's houses. I slid down the ladder and dashed towards the house. The creeper was closing in fast as I held my sword tight. I met the creeper face to face and slashed at it. It started making a creepy sizzling sound so I backed off. The creeper became quiet and started making its way towards me. I started to panic and swung my sword wildly at it. The creeper fell over in defeat. It disappeared into a bunch of sparkling green lights. That was my first win and it felt great! I was going to become a powerful warrior!

Before heading home I looked around one more time for any other invaders. The night seemed silent so I felt it safe to head on home. The villager that owned that house thanked me from his door as I walked by.

That was my day, book and quill, hope you liked it. Oh, there was one more thing I wanted to write about!

There is a girl who lives in my village named Alex. She is so amazingly beautiful. My eyes just gravitate towards her in a crowd. There is something about her. No, that is not because she is the only one different among all the villagers. She is special in another way. Maybe it is the way her hair flows in the wind. Maybe it is the way she is so kind to the villagers. I did not see her today sadly. She must have gone and visited our neighbor town. I really want to have a friend other than the squids. After that fight I had today I feel brave and strong. Tomorrow I will work up the courage to go talk to her!

Tumbling Tuesday

I got a great story to tell today Book and Quill. Remember those creepers from last night? Well, it was not the last we seen of them. We almost never get creeper sightings around here but all of a sudden they are showing up, more than one at a time. I am writing this in the safety of the church, so do not worry. It would suck if I got blown up while writing. Let me start at the beginning of the day, when I woke up.

I hate being woken up early, sleeping is one of my favorite times of the day. What woke me up were voices from the villagers outside. "Why are there creepers coming to our remote village!?" One of the villagers said. At this point I decided to go outside to see what the entire ruckus is about.

"One of them blew up part of my farm yesterday!" A villager farmer complained. I helped him out yesterday so it was sad to hear it got ruined. Another creeper must have attacked after I went to sleep last night. I tend to be a heavy sleeper sometimes.

The villager I saved yesterday came forward. "If it was not for Steve, I would have more than just a small hole near my home to worry about." It feels good to be talked about like this.

"Calm down. It is over now. We will increase the number of villagers on watch duty at night to make sure no more incidents like this happen," the priest reassured the other villagers. He then walked over to me and said, "Steve, good job last night." I just nodded back at him. "I would like to ask if you could help us watch for creepers at night. You seem reliable enough." I could not believe that the priest has finally recognized my awesome skills.

I replied fast, "Of course, Steve the warrior at your service!"

The priest nodded back. "Thank you, Steve. Also, may I ask if you go inform Alex of these events? She just got back from her trip and I worry about her." The priest did sound very worried. What was he worried about? Alex is amazing with a bow and can take care of herself.

"Yeah, I can go tell her," I accepted. He then walked back towards the church. The other villagers dispersed. I decided to head straight to Alex's house.

Alex's house is up a hill. I hate hills, so tiring. We really need to install some stairs in this village. Her house is not only better looking but bigger than mine. My house is only like nine squares inside. I really need to work on building my house bigger. Alex takes really good care of her pink flower garden. I noticed in her window there was a golden helmet hanged up. She must have gotten that on her trip. It looked so shiny, lucky her.

Before I knocked on her door, I noticed the butcher roaming around. I called out to him, "Hey Butchy!" He seemed like he was panicking. I walked over to him and noticed what he was looking at. There were two creepers hanging out beside Alex's house! They were looking at each other strangely. Butchy was frozen solid so I knew it was up to me to chase these guys away. "Butchy get out of here, I got this!" I yelled at him. That got him to his senses and he hurried off. I

pulled my iron sword out and made my way over.

"Hey creepers! Get out of my village!" I do not know if it was the smartest decision to yell at the creepers like that because afterwards they started sizzling. Just like last time I backed away but this time they stood there, looking at each other. I decided to go forward and strike the closer one with my sword. Then the other creeper charged at me. I tried to back away but I tripped. That was when it happened. BOOM! The creeper exploded right beside the house. It took the whole wall out with it. I got hit a bit from the explosion as I struggled to stand. I was then surprised to see that the second creeper did not go for me but went inside the house. This made me see that Alex was not home so why did he go inside. He then blew up inside the house. Half of the house was gone. I was baffled.

Alex came up the hill, with bread in hand, and looked at her house in astonishment. She was speechless. I walked up to her with my head held down. I was so

ashamed that I could not save her house. "I am sorry", I managed to tell her. I cannot believe the first words I ever spoke to Alex were that. I failed her. At that moment I thought she would never befriend a failure like me.

She turned her head to me and held out her bread. "Here, get your health back up." It was true; I skipped breakfast so I was too hungry to heal the wounds I got from the blast. I nodded as I took the bread and munched on it. She looked back at her devastated house. "At least most of my flowers survived." I could not tell if she was being optimistic about the situation or if she really did not care.

I finished eating the bread. "I really tried to get rid of the creepers but I messed up badly." I frowned. I could not even look at her so I put my head down and looked at the dirt.

"It's okay Steve. I can tell you tried," she put her hand on my shoulder as she said that. "I will just have to build it back up better than ever before." Alex is just so nice!

"I will help you then!" I really wanted to make it up to her for messing up.

Alex went and started picking up the remains of her house. Then she said, "I am just wondering why there are creepers during the day."

I went and helped her. As I remembered my reason for being here I shouted, "Oh yeah!" I looked over to Alex. "I came here to warn you about an increase of creeper sightings at night. This is the first time they struck in daylight though," I explained to her, "It is also weird how they ignored me. Almost like they wanted to destroy your house, like it was their mission."

She said, "Oh wow, how scary!" It was a very scary thing to think about. She placed down a chest near her ruined bed. At least she still had half of it left I thought. I would never say that out loud though. "I wonder if there are going to be more creepers," she said worryingly.

We started putting the remains into the chest. "I don't know," I told her. I looked towards the mountain. For now there was no more to be seen. "I wonder if they are all coming from the same place."

Alex held out some wood while looking around at her ruined house. "Well I am going to get started on repairing this before nightfall. How about you go ask around if anybody saw where they came from." I liked her idea, a good old fashion investigation. If I could find where they come from and stop them at the source then I could be a true hero to the village. I stood there, day dreaming about being a hero as Alex started placing some wood flooring down. "Um, Steve? Maybe you should get going now?" I snapped back into reality and noticed I was standing on dirt with wood all around me. I was just in her way there.

"Hehehe, sure," I chuckled as I jumped up and out of the way. "Leave the investigation to me!"

Alex looked at me unimpressed. "You are only interviewing a couple villagers." I chuckled again, embarrassed. I hurried away, through the half opened wall that used to have a door. Then I tripped again as I was leaving, making me even more embarrassed.

My first villager I needed to interview was the butcher. He was there at the scene of the crime! I was really getting into the whole detective role. I found him at his shop, typical. Then I approached him looking for answers. "Butchy!"

I seemed to of spooked him cause he jumped back and span around in circles for a moment. "It wasn't my fault!" He screamed.

I looked at him confused. "I was not saying it was. I just came here to ask if you knew where those creepers came from."

He settled down and took a big sigh. "Yeah, I did see them approaching. I really wanted to fight them myself but I chickened out." Butchy looked ashamed. That was why

I saw him frozen at the scene of the crime. It was not like I did any better though.

If I wanted answers, I was going to have to cheer him up first. "It's okay Butchy. It is the thought that counts. Besides, two creepers are just too much for one villager to handle." If someone helped me out, maybe I could have saved Alex's house. I could not blame him for that though.

"Thanks Steve," he said with his frown turned upside down.

"So can you tell me if you know where they came from?" I asked him again.

The Butcher stood, thinking for a moment. "Oh! I remember they came from the mountain. You should also go ask the farmer who had his crops destroyed. He was raging on about the mountain being a nest of creepers. That is why nobody is going out there and I am getting little supply of ore." The butcher had been very helpful so I thanked him and hurried on to go interview my next target, the farmer.

I found the farmer farming away at his ruined field. I felt bad for the poor guy so I decided to help him. "So, could you tell me what happened here?" I asked him as I started placing the dirt around the water so it stopped flowing like crazy.

The farmer stood up and brushed off his sweat from his forehead as he said, "Hey Steve. Thanks for the help. What happened here was horrible." I could see the pained expression on the poor farmer's face, like he ate a poisoned potato. "I was just minding my own business, getting ready for bed, when I looked out the window to my farm. That is when I saw a creeper creeping up on my crops. I thought it would be fine because I hear they only cause trouble if you approach them. That thought was completely wrong. Out of nowhere he started making those weird sounds and blew up. My poor crops that were almost ready to be harvested were ruined. There was not even anybody around so why would it do that. It is a madness I say, madness!" The farmer started freaking out.

I finished playing in the dirt and stood up. "I see. So the creeper destroyed your crops with no warning. You saw this from your window so you could not of seen where it came from then," I deduced.

"Oh I know where they came from!" He started talking with a crazy expression. "It is that cursed mountain that we mined all the minerals from! My brother is a miner and works for the blacksmith. He comes home and tells me about all the creepers he sees over there. There are hoards and hoards of them he says! I have not seen him in a couple days since the last time he headed out towards the mountain." I was wondering why I have not seen his brother around in a while. "Steve, you got to believe me! Something is going on up there!" Is this guy a nut case or what?

I decided to go along with what he said for now. "Alright, I will see what I can find out about this mountain." I told him.

"Please, find my brother!" The farmer yelled out as I started to leave.

"I will do my best!" I yelled back to him. There was one more villager I needed to interview before I reported back to Alex. That villager was the one I saved last night. I headed towards his house. Soon I will wrap up this mystery and show off to Alex my greatness I thought.

The villager that I saved was a fisherman. We always loved to fish together and compete on who can fish up more. I never won though. His amazing luck felt like cheating to me. I kept fishing up junk and all he got was fish. Anyways, I found him at his house just hanging around. "Hey, how are you doing?" I asked him. The best thing to do is always be casual and not be intimidating when you want to interview someone.

"Oh hey Steve. I am doing fine," he casually replied. "Thanks for last night. That creeper was sure scary."

"No problem! So about last night, did you by any chance see where that creeper came from?"

"Yeah I did actually." The fisherman walked over to the side of his house where the hole was. I followed. "Over there, the direction of the mountain." He pointed towards the mountain.

"From within the mines?" I asked, looking for more specific information.

"I do not know if he came from inside the mine as I could not spot him from that far away. I do know he came straight here like he was chasing something. I hurried inside to protect myself when he started getting close." It is the correct instinct to hide in doors. Creepers are not supposed to attack unless you are seen. They usually have very short view range so there is no way the

24

creeper from all the way at the mountain would lock on to a villager all the way here.

"Thank you for the information." After that interview I had enough to deduct that all the creepers are coming from the mountain and are acting strange. I decided to quickly report back to Alex.

I hurried up the hill as the sun was going down. "Alex, I have returned!" I announced.

I was looking around but could not see Alex. "Over here!" I heard her call from around the house. I went over and saw her working over a crafting table. "I am just making some more arrows in case more creepers show up." That was a very wise decision. "So what is the conclusion of your investigation?" She got straight to the point.

"Well apparently they are coming from the mountain. All the creeper cases were weird, so they are not acting normal." I summarized for her.

"So nothing useful then?" she said bluntly. That kind of hurt but it was true I could not truly understand the reason for these creepers coming and wreaking havoc. I also could not find their exact location.

This was when I made my epic decision. "Well that is why tomorrow I am going to go to the mountain and figure this out with my own two blocky hands," I stated. Most of all, I really wanted to get revenge on these creepers for ruining Alex's house and making me look bad. "I will go as soon as the sun rises! Oh but the priest told me to help keep watch over the town tonight so looks like I am pulling an all-nighter." I stayed up all night before while reading a good book or watching the night sky on my roof. This time is different though, I would be using much more energy than usual.

"My bow and I will help you then!" She put her arrows away and pulled out her bow. She looked tough but stunning at the same time.

I quickly shook my head to gain composure. "I can't let myself put a girl in harm's way! What kind of man would I be?" I really wanted to show her my tough side.

"I think I can take out more with my bow then your little iron sword." Her sass also made her look cute. "Besides, if we take turns on lookout then we can both get some rest for the journey tomorrow."

I had to think about that for a moment. Did she just assume she was coming on the journey with me? I had to ask. "Wait, you wanted to come tomorrow to the mountain with me?"

"Of course I am coming. Two is better than one. I also had my share of journeys so I am tougher than I look," she said with confidence.

The sun was almost gone now and all the villagers started heading indoors. "Well we better head to high ground then to get a good lookout going." She nodded as she quickly grabbed a couple of carrots. Snacks are the best when you do not want to fall asleep. "To the church!" I shouted as I lead the way

We headed to the top of the church and waited for the moon to rise. Alex looked stunning in the light of the moon. She looked over at me and caught me staring. I looked away embarrassed. "If you're not going to actually look out, then you can go to sleep. I will take the first watch and wake you when it is your turn."

I could not let her show me up. "No, it is okay. You had a long trip back so I will let you sleep first. You can count on me!" She shrugged and nodded. She took me up on my offer and headed down to the middle floor of the church to rest.

So this is where I am at now, writing in you, book and quill. The night is peaceful and there was only a couple zombies spotted in the distance. They always burn away in the morning so no need to bug them. My eyes are getting heavy now as the moon reaches the top of the sky. I decided it was time to switch with Alex.

Wacky Wednesday

Today we started on our journey towards the mountain. I packed light with a few pieces of bread. All I really needed was my trusty iron sword and my shield. I showed off my shield to Alex but she did not look impressed. "Why did you not use that shield against the creepers yesterday?" she asked me as I was practicing my guarding.

My shield was hand crafted by me and it was hard to make. "I do not want my shield getting exploded by a creeper, took me forever to make this!" I believed that the shield was only good for deflecting arrows and zombie punches.

Alex had finished packing her share of food along with her bow and arrows. "It's only wood and an iron ingot," She mumbled. Well that one iron ingot was the first one I ever smelted! We started walking away from the village. "But, you do know that the shield can resist the creeper's blast right?" I looked at her amazed. Alex was not only beautiful but smart too.

Not wanting to look like I do not know anything, I made up an excuse. "Yeah, but it still damages the shield. I got to make it last!"

"Whatever you say shield lover," she chuckled.

I still could not believe I was going on adventure with Alex. I looked behind me as the village became smaller, and then looked back ahead to the mountain that seemed to be growing. "Come on let's go!" I said as I hurried up the pace.

We arrived at the mountain and found the mine that we would get minerals from. I first made sure there were no creepers or other monsters around before leading the way inside. Alex was the archer so she stayed behind me and my trusty shield. We made our way down and saw that some torches had fallen on the ground. It was dangerous to continue in the dark so we put them back up as went along. After around the 10th fallen torch, we started hearing sounds of zombies. We readied our weapons and met them as they came around a dark corner. I let Alex shoot them first before I moved in and struck the final blow. "Yay, we did it!" I shouted as we beat the two zombies.

"Shh!" Alex shushed me, "I hear more, maybe spiders this time." She was right. I heard spiders coming down the same corridor. It sounded like multiple of them.

All of a sudden we heard a voice of a villager. "Is somebody there!? Help me!" The villager cried out. Then I remembered the farmer telling me his brother had not come back from the mines. I wondered if that was him.

I looked over at Alex. "We got to help him," I told her.

"Of course, let's squash those bugs!" She replied as she rushed ahead.

I hurried behind. "Hey watch out!" A spider came from an above passage and dropped down behind her. This was not a normal spider, it was a cave spider. They could inflict poison if they get you. I knew she could not prepare her arrow fast enough so I lunged at the spider. Stabbing it before it could reach her. My iron sword was not strong enough to vanquish it in one blow. The spider got me and I could feel the poison eating away at my health. I swung again and killed it.

Alex hurried back over to me. "I am so sorry. I should not have run off like that." Alex looked at me so worryingly. It felt nice to have her worry about me.

"I am not going to die am I?" I asked her, scared for myself. The poison hurt all over. This is why I made sure not to eat any poisonous potatoes.

"No it won't kill you but here have some carrots to keep your health up as it fades away." Alex shared some carrots she packed with me. Sure made me wish for a nice warm baked potato. As I finished eating the poison went away and I felt better. "You okay now?" She asked as she kept watch on the tunnel the spider came from.

I said, "Yeah!" I was a warrior and no warrior goes down this easily. A couple more spiders started to emerge from the tunnel and Alex shot them all down before they reached us. "We need to get up to that tunnel to stop the spiders at the source." As she kept shooting down any spiders that came for us, I started digging some dirt away to make a path up. Then I reached some stone that was too hard for my poor hands to handle. "Uh oh," I said out loud.

"You did not pack a pickaxe? Fine, use mine then," she said as she quickly took out her pickaxe and tossed it over to me. I picked it up and started mining away at the stone. "Are you done yet?" She was not only getting low on patience but low on arrows too.

I mined away the last piece of stone and made a path. "There, let's go!" I shouted as another spider came my way and I jumped

back. Alex shot it and I hurried upwards. There were no more spiders and I could see the monster spawner that they came from.

This was my chance and I charged ahead. I got caught in a spider web as I tried to reach the spawner. "Ahhh," I cried out as I wiggled around trying to break free.

"Use your sword!" Alex told me as she came up the path I made. Dangling in a web like that in front of her was sure embarrassing.

I swung my sword around wildly and managed to break the web. "I'm free!" Alex killed another spider that spawned as I started breaking all the webs leading to the spawner. Did I mention that her accuracy was spot on? Well it was. She was an amazing archer.

I tried to kill the spawner with my sword but it was not working very well. "Use the pickaxe!" Alex shouted out to me. I quickly switched to the pickaxe and made quick work of the spawner. I looked back at Alex who was collecting some string from the webs. "This string is good for making new bows" she said. I felt disappointed. It was not like I wanted her to praise me or anything but a simple good job still would have been nice.

As I sighed, I heard the villager's voice again. "You killed the spiders?" He asked. His voice was closer.

I answered back to him, "yep! All safe now"!

The villager appeared from behind some dirt. "Thank you. These spiders chased me and I have been hiding in a dirt tunnel for a couple days now." He looked over at Alex who started eating a carrot. "Foooood," he groaned. He must have been hungry because it was not only his mouth talking but his stomach too.

"Here have some of my bread," I said to him as I offered out one of my bread.

He quickly took it and gobbled it up. "Thank you so much Steve, you are my hero," he praised me. There, that was the praise I longed for.

"No problem," I replied, trying not to show how happy I was for being called a hero. "Your brother is worried about you back at the village," I told him.

"Thanks, I will head back now," he said as he started leaving.

"Wait!" I stopped him before he left, "I wanted to ask if you knew anything about the creepers. There have been a lot of them attacking the village since you been gone."

"Yeah I remember seeing a lot of them on top of the mountain. They would come and go from the other side," the villager answered.

"So they do not come from within the mines?" I clarified.

"Nope, hardly see them down here," the villager replied again.

"Thank you for the information," I said to him as he nodded and ran out of the mines. I looked back over to Alex who was now getting some flint from nearby gravel. "So I guess our journey will take us past the mountain now."

Alex finished and headed back down the path I made. "Good, I was starting to get tired of this gloomy cave," she said happily. I agreed with her and followed her out of the cave. It was almost time for the sun to go down. We were in the mines longer then I thought. Alex pulled out a map, "We can stay tonight at the desert village at the edge of the taiga on the other side of this mountain." I nodded as I followed her directions. Good thing she had a map, I might have gotten lost on my own.

I made sure to keep looking around the mountain area as we headed to the village. There was no sign of any creepers around which felt strange. We took shelter in one of the vacant houses in the village. What a wacky day it has been.

Thrilling Thursday

When I woke up today, I noticed Alex was not around. I headed outside and took a look around. It was a small desert village. Most of all, it was so hot! How can anyone handle this heat? I heard some villagers talking so I headed towards them. They were gathered around the well. "Yes, I saw a creeper come from the desert temple!" one of the villagers said. I then noticed that they were all talking to Alex, so I walked over to her.

"Hey, already doing some investigation?" I asked her.

"Yes, I thought you could use some more sleep so I went ahead," she said with care in her voice. Aw, how thoughtful is she!

"Thanks!" I replied, "So what did you find out?"

She turned her attention to the villagers and said, "Thanks guys, I got all the information I need," before turning back to me. "It seems like they are coming from the desert temple." The last villager did say he saw a creeper come from there. I am so amazed she got all the information she needed already, while I took a whole day to only find out to check the mountain. She continued, "They seem to avoid this village and go straight over the mountain."

Why would they not attack this village but attack ours? This was a strange mystery that I was eager to solve. "Then let's check out this temple!" I ordered. Then I pointed my sword out to the sky and started walking forward.

I did not hear Alex follow behind me so I stopped and looked back. She said, "Um, the temple is not that way." I put my sword away and laughed off the embarrassment. "Come on, I will lead the way this time," she said as she went the opposite direction. I followed her. I would follow this girl anywhere.

As we turned around the corner of a house, I spotted a bunny. It was so cute! I went up to it and offered it a carrot. The bunny nibbled on the carrot. "Aww," I could not help but say. I then noticed that I was not showing a very manly side of me to Alex. Then I slowly turned my head to see Alex with her arms folded and a look that told me,

"Steve is so lame". I tried to redeem myself and stood up. "Hey bunny, I am too busy and too cool to help you out right now," I said with, what I thought was, a cool sounding voice. Alex rolled her eyes and turned her back on me. With her not looking at me

anymore, I quickly patted the cute bunny before following her into the desert.

While we trekked through the scorching hot desert, I could feel we were being watched. "Hey Alex, don't you feel like someone is watching us?" I asked.

The sun was bearing down on us so hard that I was struggling to walk but Alex always kept walking like it did not even bother her. Maybe she was used to the desert, or maybe I am just not as strong as her. "Yes, I can feel it too."

We went past an empty desert well which made us feel thirsty. Good thing we brought some water bottles. As we drank we kept our eyes out as we walked. Then we saw it. What we felt watching us were creepers! Their gazes were locked on us, it was pretty creepy. No pun intended. "Do you think we are getting close to their hide out?" I asked Alex. She was watching our surroundings very seriously.

She looked back at me. "Yeah, according to the villagers it is just over that river," she told me, "Watch out!" She shot an arrow towards me that just brushed against my shoulder. Startled, I quickly look behind. There was a creeper coming towards me and Alex saved me by pushing it away with an arrow.

Time to show off more of my heroic side! "Take this!" I said as I charged at the creeper. I gave it a nice hit with my iron sword and it did the job. "Thanks for that save Alex," I thanked her as I turned back. There was another creeper heading towards Alex from behind her this time. It was like the first creeper was only a decoy! I screamed out as I rushed towards her, "Alex, behind you!" It was too late for her to get away as the creeper was already making the sounds like it was going to explode any moment. Then I remembered that my shield can protect against the blast. I hurried in front of her and took out my shield. The creeper exploded as I held my shield firmly. "Phew," I said as I let my shield down.

I looked back at Alex who was safe and sound. I was ready to hear her say "you're my hero". It never happened though.

Alex only put her hand on my shoulder and said, "You finally made good use of your shield, nice." Then she walked past me. I shook off the disappointed look on my face and walked along with her.

We made it to the river without any more creepers coming after us. All they did was watch us like we were a zoo attraction. "So do we just swim across?" I asked as I looked at the river.

Before saying anything, Alex jumped right in. "The water feels great, jump in!" She called out.

It was very hot and a nice swim would feel great I thought. I decided to jump in after her. "Wow, this does feel great!" I said as I started swimming around. Alex was swimming around too. She was a good swimmer like a squid, a good-looking squid. When I looked away for a second she disappeared. I glanced around and then she popped up from below and splashed me. "Whoa."

Alex started to laugh as she said "gotcha". It looked like she was actually having fun. Here I thought Alex was always serious and did not know how to have fun. I was learning more and more about her. It really felt like we were becoming friends. I laughed along with her and splashed her back. We played in the water for a while, splashing each other. Then Alex looked up to the sky and said, "We better get going now. I believe it is best we make some shelter and wait till midnight. Most of their activity is done at night and the fewer creepers in the temple; the better."

I looked at her confused. "But I thought we came here to get rid of all the creepers?"

"No, we came here to kill the one controlling all the creepers, their leader," she answered.

"Oh, that makes sense," I said. There she goes again, being so smart. I wanted to show her that I was smart too. "So we will surprise them in the middle of the night. We will jump down through the top of the temple and surprise them even more!" It seemed like a good plan to me at the time.

Alex got out of the water and started squeezing out the water from her long and pretty orange hair. She looked sparkling as she came out of the water. "Why would we do that?" she asked, sounding not impressed with my idea.

I backed up my idea and told her, "If we get them from behind then we can more easily kill them." I started getting out of the river as I waited for her reply.

"If we just jump down into them then we might end up getting surrounded. The temple is also a small enclosed space, which means harder to escape from their exploding." My idea did not sound good after she said that. I sighed heavily. "Instead we will first try to lure out any of the creepers that are inside," she started to explain; "It will be easier to kill them out in the open. When the coast is clear we go in and investigate." Sounded like a great plan to me. I felt like a dummy for thinking my plan was good.

We headed away from the river and spotted the temple. "There it is, and the sun is going down too," I said as I squinted looking at the sun. "What now?"

"Now we make shelter and wait," Alex said as she started collecting sand.

Now I can show off to Alex by building a wonderful sand igloo I thought. I started piling the sand up, beside a sand mountain where no enemies were around, but every time I tried to make a roof it would cave in. I looked over to Alex to see her packing 4 sands together to create some sandstone. She walked over and placed it as the roof. "I was going to do that..." I said as my voice trailed off quietly.

As we finished the sand igloo, we headed on in. We took turns taking a nap as we waited for the right time to strike. I am writing this as Alex sleeps next to me. She looks so cute in her sleep, like a baby bunny that you want to protect.

Frightening Friday

The day began not with the morning sun but with gentle hands shaking me awake. "Urrrrgh," I groaned. I really wanted to sleep more. Who likes being woken up in the middle of the night?

The gentle hands started not being gentle anymore as they shook me harder. "Wake up, it's time to go," Alex said. I decided to wake up despite being tired enough to sleep through an earthquake.

I sat up and looked over at Alex. "Anything happen while I was sleeping?" I asked. She shook her head as she started grabbing her bow and arrows. I grabbed my sword and shield and crawled out of the igloo to stretch. The moon was just passing the center of the sky. Alex came out after me and started looking around. She looked beautiful under the moonlight. "Well let's get this mission over with," as I looked around cautiously with her, "no creepers in sight."

Alex started to sneak around the mountain. I followed her lead and crouched with her. We slowly approached the temple. We could see only two creepers from our angle, one inside the temple and another on top. "Let me take out the top one first," Alex said as she loaded an arrow onto her bow. She pulled the strings back and fired at the creeper. The creeper got struck and looked around confused. She fired another one which pushed the creeper off the edge. We could hear it die from the fall damage. "Next let's lure the other one outside."

Alex needed a better shot at the creeper inside so we crawled a bit closer. Then we started to hear voices. It was not the usual creeper sounds but actual words we could understand. "The creeper scouts spotted the two strange looking villagers heading our way yesterday but we lost sight of them last night," we heard the voice say.

We decided to stay hidden and listen in on their conversation. "Well find them! The whole point in attacking their village was to get rid of them!" another voice said, sounding very angry. Alex and I looked at each other surprised. They were not after destroying the village but after us. What did they want us for? The same voice started talking again, "I am going back to my secret

lair. The next time I come out I better see their heads on a stick." Wow, scary huh?

"Yes sir," the same voice from before said. I heard some blocks moving around and then it was silent.

Alex and I nodded at each other, signaling it was time to strike. I Jumped inside the temple door and waved the sword around. "Hey creeper, come and get me!" I shouted at him as he looked at me with the usual ugly looking creeper face. I lured him outside so Alex could strike him as he came out of the entrance. Then I finished the job with a blow to the head. This time, as the creeper disappeared, he left his head on the ground. I picked it up and looked at it. "Hey this could be useful. We could pretend to be a creeper." I placed the creeper head on. It was weird looking through the eyes of a creeper. I started making creeper sounds.

"Stop playing around," said Alex. I pouted as I took the head off. "I wonder if this creeper was one of the ones talking." The thought of creepers talking, that sounded crazy!

"The only way to find out,"—I put the creeper head away and entered the temple—"is to find the other one that was talking."

Alex followed me inside and we cautiously looked around. The insides were nicely made and I wondered who build it. I decided to ask Alex, "Who do you think built these temples anyways? Was it the creepers or did the villagers build it then abandon it?"

"If you paid attention in history class then you would have heard the theory of an ancient civilization called Creepgyptians that lived in the desert. They built these places to live in but there were no records in what happened to them." Wow, if history was this interesting I should have fallen asleep less.

After investigating around and looking up and down the stairs, we deduced there were no more creepers around. Alex kept looking around as she was still not convinced. One of the voices did say he had a secret lair after all. I noticed the pretty colored blocks in the center as the light from the rising sun shined through the top of the temple. Walking up to them I tripped and fell. With my face to the floor I heard sounds coming from beneath the temple. Who knew that by tripping I could find a clue! "Hey, Alex, over here," I called Alex over. She also put her face to the ground and heard the sounds. "Let's try digging down," I suggested. Alex nodded and I tried mining the center block.

Before the cracks fully destroyed the block, Alex stopped me and said "wait." I looked at her confused as she got up and moved back to the block beside. "Try mining the one beside it. The middle one just seems too suspicious."

I went along with what she said and mined the one beside it. To our surprise, the block fell down a dark hole. We waited for a couple seconds to hear the sound of it reaching the bottom. It did not take too long so we knew it was not that deep. "How do we get down?" I asked Alex.

"I will build some ladders; you take this coal and craft us some torches," she directed. After passing me coal I took out the last of my wood and made some sticks. I ignited the sticks with the coal to turn them into torches. I watched Alex as she placed down a crafting table and built some ladders.

Once we were prepared we slowly descended the hole, ladder at a time. Alex went first, placing the ladders. I then followed, placing the torches. By working together we made it to the bottom. Before taking a step towards the center of the small space, Alex put her arm out to stop me. "What's wrong?" I asked.

"Look down," she replied.

I looked down and saw a pressure plate. It could have been a trap. "Good call on not digging at the center, it would have landed on this pressure plate."

For all we knew, it could have blown the whole place up. As I thought that Alex said, "Creepers sure do love their explosions." It was like she read my mind!

Now that we knew not to step on the pressure plate we finally took a good look around. There were three chests on the floor.

"Do you think the chests are booby traps too?" I asked her as I examined a chest.

"We better not touch them, better safe than sorry."

"Yeah, you're right." Alex is always right. I was so curious what was in them but I had to listen to Alex. It is like getting a present on your birthday but you are not allowed to open it.

"Look, there's a door. Maybe the other voice we heard went this way," Alex said as she tried to look through the door's window. "I do not see anybody so let's go in."

"Let me go first with my shield." I carefully moved around the pressure plate. Alex gently opened the door for me to walk through. She followed behind me as she closed the door.

We walked slowly down a long corridor. "Be careful," Alex whispered.

We reached another door at the end. This door was made of iron and could not be opened by hand. We needed to find a button or leaver so we looked around. "How are we going to open—Oh look!" I spotted two leavers on the roof of the corridor. "One could be another trap while the other will open the door," I said as I thought of the 50:50 chance we could get blown up.

"I remember reading a sign posted on the stairway I checked." Alex said the sign wrote, "Remember to press the lever that is farther away from the door." What a useful sign, telling any intruders how to open the door. Does that not defeat the purpose of having the trap in the first place? Alex added, "There was another sign beside it that said 'or get exploded by an explosion that is not your own'." How nice.

We pressed the correct switch and the iron door opened. We cautiously went through. On the other side was a dark looking room. On one side it had tables and chairs. It looked like a nice place to relax. From the walls hanged banners with the face of a creeper on it. It was probably the creeper gang's hang out area.

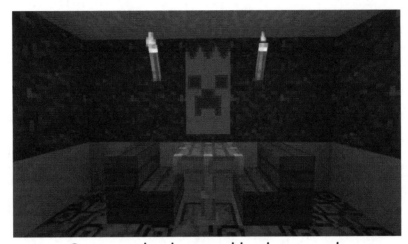

Once we had a good look around us, we both noticed something green emerging from the banners in the back of the room. A familiar voice came through, "I see you brats have made it all the way here." The voice we heard earlier, that seemed like the boss, belonged to a creeper! The creeper stood in front of us on top of a stone slap. "This is where your journey comes to an end." He sure sounded menacing.

Alex took a fierce step forward and asked, "Are you behind all the creeper attacks!?"

"Maybe I am, Maybe I'm not," the creeper replied.

I also took a step forward and said, "If you are or not does not matter because we are going to bring a stop to all of your exploding."

"You are now?" The creeper slowly advanced towards us. "I would like to see you try!"

"Let's get him Alex!" I charged forward with my sword and struck him as hard as I could. My sword broke on impact as the durability was no more. I had nothing but my shield to protect me now.

The creeper crept closer towards me. "I am going to get you now!"

"No you don't!" Alex shot the creeper with an arrow, pushing him back. "Oh no, that was my last arrow."

The creeper laughed evilly. I thought; what do we do now? I lost my iron sword and Alex had no more arrows. We could let him explode himself as we have my shield. This was a talking creeper though. He may not have just a normal explosion. The creeper kept getting closer as we backed away. We were running out of time.

I looked around the room for answers and noticed a trap door. There was a button over at the wall that might be able to activate it. I nudged Alex towards the direction of the button. She nodded and made her way over there. She was going to press the button and I needed to get the creeper on the door. "Come and get me you ugly creeper!" I taunted him as I put the trap door in between me and him. I held my shield up to make him think I was going to take his blast.

"No shield will protect you now!" He said as he came closer.

The creeper finally stepped on top of the trap door. I shouted "Now!" Alex pressed the button and the creeper fell through.

We rushed over to see him falling down. "How could I forget my own traaaap," the creeper cried out as the sound of his voice drowned away. He dropped into a pool of lava at the bottom of the hole. Well that was the end of that. I thought it felt a little anti-climactic.

Alex headed for the door. "Let's blow up this temple and get out of here."

"Wait!" I called out, "there is a chest over here." I wanted to at least take some treasure back. "This chest probably belongs to that boss sounding creeper so it must hold some goodies."

"Sure, go ahead. This chest looks fine to me." Alex waited at the door.

I carefully opened the chest and peeked inside. The sparkle of a diamond caught my eye. I fully opened the chest and screamed out "diamonds!" I grabbed the diamonds and a written book that was there. I met up with Alex and we left the room. Goodbye creepy creeper lair I thought as we walked down the corridor.

We came back to the room with the suspicious looking chests. "Can't believe these creepers changed this desert temple to be their hide out," Alex said.

I let Alex climb the ladder first and followed behind. We reached the top and I took out Alex's pickaxe that she gave me. "Do you want to do the honors?" I asked her as I held the pickaxe out to her.

"I would love to"—she grabbed the pickaxe— "but get ready to run." I headed to the temple door as she mined the center blue block. As soon as she finished mining, she

hurried over. The block started to fall as we ran outside. We heard the explosion behind us. We turned around to see the ruined temple.

We took a moment to look at what we had done. "I kind of feel bad that we destroyed something that's been around for so long," I said.

"Yeah," said Alex.

"Oh well." I turned around and headed away.

"Let's rest before we make the long way back home," Alex suggested. I agreed and we headed back to our sand igloo.

What a thrilling day it had been Book and Quill. We took down the evil creeper organization and exploded a desert temple. Tomorrow we will make our way back home to be crowned heroes.

Stormy Saturday

Today we made our way back to our village. Sadly it was storming out. I made the wrong choice of going over the mountain on our way back. Alex skillfully dodged a lightning bolt. "Wow amazing!" I told her. As I was shocked at how amazing she was, I got shocked myself. She just laughed at me as I ate my, now toasted, bread. It was a tiring journey back so that is all I am going to write today my book and quill. Hopefully tomorrow, which will be our welcome back and celebration party, will be sunny. I am so excited like a child villager getting a rose from an iron golem. Hmm, note to shelf, build an iron golem to help protect the village next time we are getting attacked.

Sunny Sunday

Today I woke up to the morning sun. I rolled over to my side and this time Alex was not around. I already missed having her around. After getting sad for a moment I remembered that today we should be celebrating the end of the creepers. It got me excited again as I hopped out of bed. I quickly ate a light breakfast of one baked potato. I sure did miss the taste of a freshly baked potato. Then I hurried off to the center of town.

Most of the villagers were gathered around the well. I waved to them and said, "Hey everyone!"

They looked over to me and all of a sudden surrounded me. I was almost ready for them to pick me up and throw me in the air while cheering or something. "You did it Steve! No more creepers have shown up last night. I heard from Alex you destroyed their hide out," the priest was saying, "I knew we could count on you."

"Yeah Steve, good job," the butcher added. It felt great to be told you did a good

job.

An orange cat pushed its way past the librarian and meowed. "I even got a cat to help chase away any more creepers, just in case," the librarian said. I thought to myself, so much for being confident in me.

"You even saved my brother," the farmer said.

"Yes, I am very thankful to you and Alex," said the brother.

"Speaking of Alex, where is she?" I asked the villagers.

The fisherman replied, "I saw her relaxing by the water."

"Thanks, I am going to go see what she is up to." I turned to start heading toward the water.

"Wait," the priest said, stopping me, "we all wanted to give you a present. For Alex, we rebuilt her golden helmet and parts of her house. This is what we made for you." The priest handed me a frame with a golden sword inside. A sword made of gold! I totally hanged the frame in my room and I am admiring it even now. It was also nice of the villagers to rebuild Alex's home and make her that golden helmet. I never did ask how she got a golden helmet in the first place.

"Thanks!" I thanked all the villagers and waved them goodbye. Then I hurried off to go see Alex by the water.

I found Alex fishing at the end of the pier. "Catch anything?" I asked casually.

She replied, "Only some string." I am glad I am not the only one that fishes out junk. "Did you see the villagers? They were so nice to me," she said as I sat beside her and pulled my own fishing rod out.

"Yep, they even gave me this amazing framed golden sword," I told her.

"Wow, how did they manage to get gold?"

I laughed. "We did great, didn't we?" I wondered if she saw me as a cool hero now.

"Yeah, I guess so." Why did Alex always feel so lack luster to our achievements?

I wanted to know so I asked her, "Don't you think were amazing heroes now?" I paused and swallowed before I continued, "Why is it that no matter how hard I try to impress you, you never seem to notice."

Alex looked over at me as she finished wheeling in a name tag. She sighed. I do not know if that sigh was from not fishing up a fish or if it was from what I said. "I already knew you were very capable. I always watched you help around the town. Saw you practicing your sword skills behind your house. I would not have teamed up with you if I thought you were useless."

"So you already thought I was amazing?"

Alex laughed. "Yes Steve, I always thought you were amazing. You did not have to act like a hero to show that to me."

I scratched my head as I blushed. So I was not just watching her from a distance but she was also watching me. I had to ask one more thing, "So, are we friends now?"

Alex replied, "Of course we are, friends and partners of justice."

I laughed. "You are my partner with the all the smarts, Alex the archer."

She laughed along with me, "And you are the courageous partner, Steve the warrior."

As we were laughing, I got a bite on my fishing rod. I quickly wheeled it in and at the end of the line was a glowing book. "Oh wow, who would throw this in the water?" I examined it. "I wonder what a power enchant is."

"That's for increasing bow damage."

"Oh, then here. I'll let you have it." I tossed the book over to Alex. This was my first present I gave to her.

"Thanks," she said as she took the book. "You also got a book from that creeper lair didn't you?"

I almost forgot about that. After putting my fishing rod away, I took out the written book that I was still holding on to. "Let me read it out loud," I said, "it reads; 'I am writing down my mission that was handed to me just in case I accidentally blow up. This is not about my anger that some other creepers like to think I have. This is about if my life comes to an end. The mission must continue. We, the creepers, were tasked to take out the weird looking villagers. They do not belong here with their nice looking hair and fashionable style. There are two of them living in the taiga village over the mountain by the water. Upon completing this mission you will gain all the creeper luxuries you want'. " What do creepers even enjoy? The last line said, "'If you fail, I will explode you all myself'." Well that did not sound good. At least we disposed of them.

Alex stood up and said, "So that final creeper was not the real boss. There is still somebody out there that gave him that mission."

"But, who could it be? Just because we have cool hair is no reason to attack us." I wondered if our adventure was only just beginning. I guess this will not be the last adventure I write in you, book and quill.

"There must be more to it than that. For now, we should strengthen the village defenses just in case." Alex looked very determined.

I stood up and shouted, "Yeah!"

We looked out into the horizon together and I wondered who else was out there. Whatever challenges we do face, we will face them together.

49194432R00045

Made in the USA
Middletown, DE
08 October 2017